THE WAY
TO
START A DAY

by BYRD BAYLOR

illustrated by PETER PARNALL

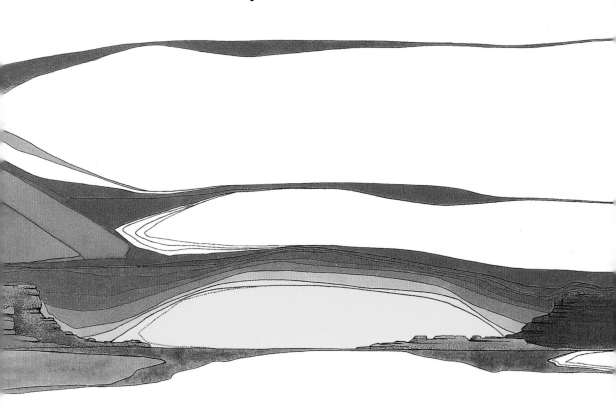

Aladdin Paperbacks

First Aladdin Paperbacks edition 1986
Revised format edition 1998

Text copyright © 1977, 1978 by Byrd Baylor
Illustrations copyright © 1978 by Peter Parnall
This text appeared in McCall's magazine, February 1977

Aladdin Paperbacks
An imprint of Simon & Schuster
Children's Publishing Division
1230 Avenue of the Americas
New York, NY 10020

Manufactured in China

30 29

Library of Congress Cataloging-in-Publication Data
Baylor, Byrd.
The way to start a day.
Reprint. Originally published: New York: C. Scribner's Sons, 1978, c1977.
"A Caldecott honor book."
Summary: Describes how people all over the world celebrate the sunrise.
1. Sun—Rising and setting—Juvenile literature.
2. Sun worship—Juvenile literature.   [1. Sun—Folklore]
I. Parnall, Peter, ill.   II. Title.
[BL325.S8B34   1986]   291.3'8   85-28802
ISBN-13: 978-0-689-71054-4 (pbk.)
ISBN-10: 0-689-71054-2 (pbk.)

0217 SCP

The way to start a day
is this—

Go outside
and face the east
and greet the sun
with some kind of
blessing
or chant
or song
that you made yourself
and keep for
early morning.

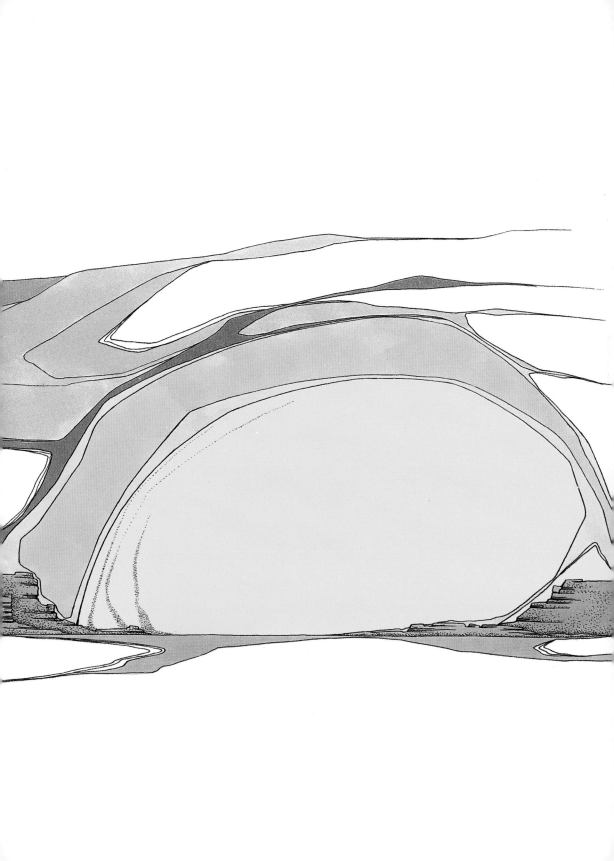

The way to make the song
is this—

Don't try to think
what words to use
until
you're standing there
alone.

When you feel the sun
you'll feel
the song too.

Just sing it.

But
don't think you're
the only one
who ever worked
that magic.

Your caveman brothers
knew what to do.
Your cavewoman sisters
knew too.
They sang
to help the sun
come up
and lifted their hands
to its power.

A morning
needs
to be sung to.
A new day
needs
to be honored.

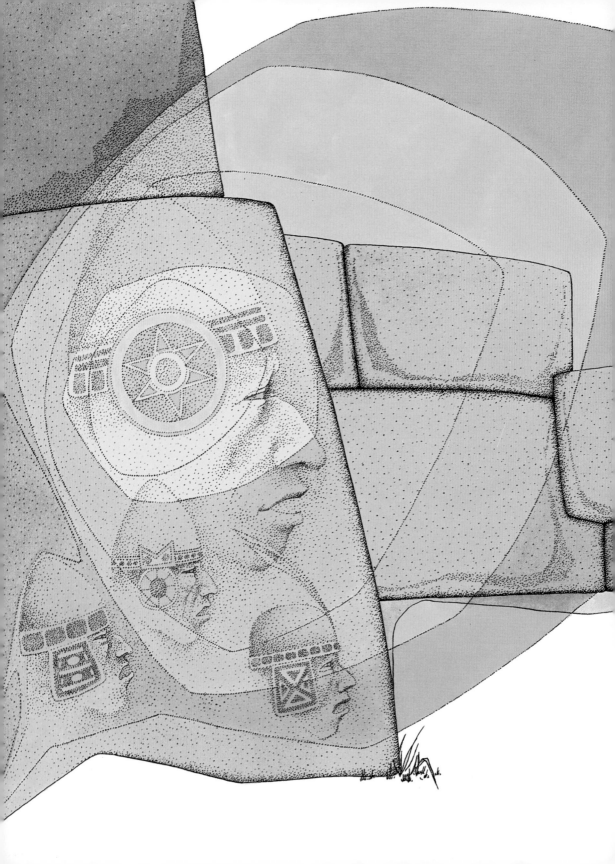

People
have always
known that.

Didn't they chant
at dawn
in the sun temples
of Peru?

And leap and sway
to Aztec flutes
in Mexico?

And drum
sunrise songs
in the Congo?

And ring
a thousand
small gold bells
in China?

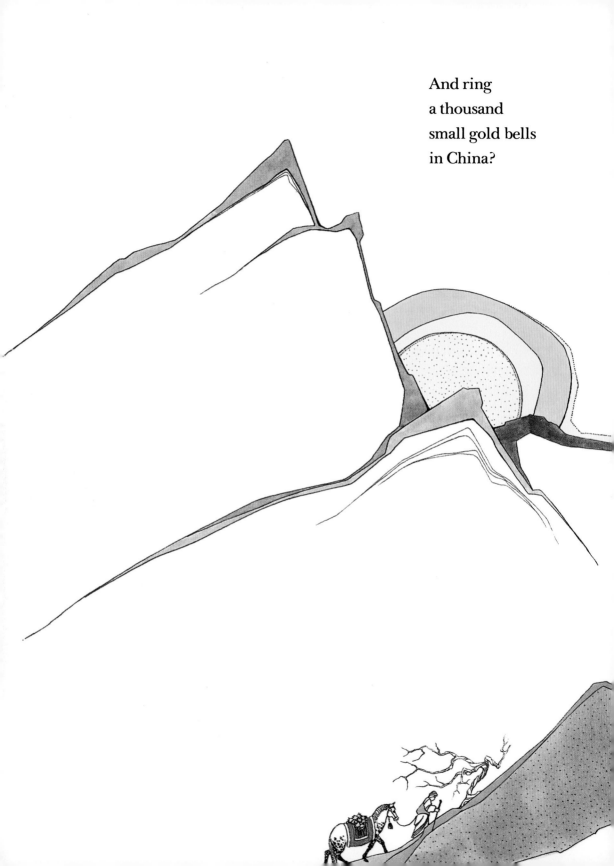

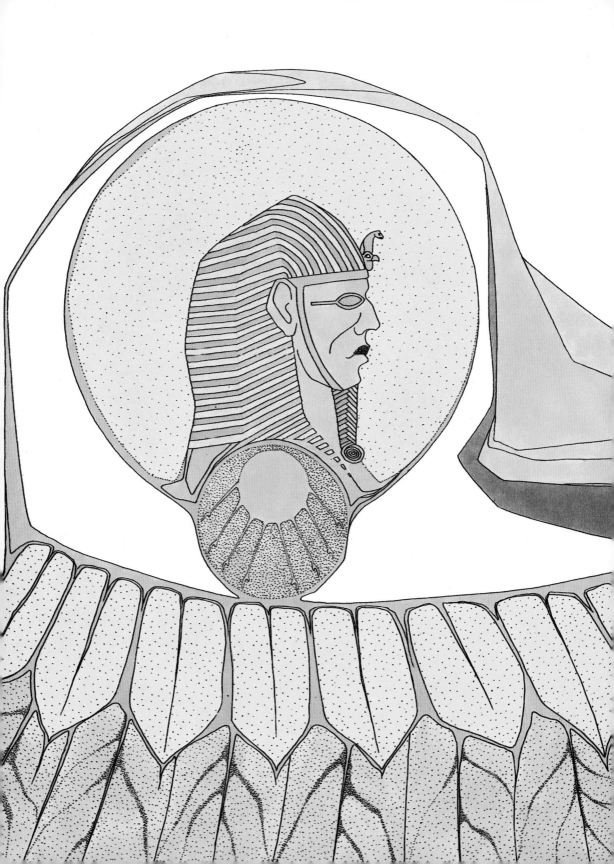

Didn't the pharaohs
of Egypt
say
the only
sound
at dawn
should be
the sound of
songs
that please
the morning sun?

They knew
what songs
to sing.

People
always
seemed to know.

And
everywhere
they knew
what gifts
the sun
wanted.

In some places
they gave
gold.
In some places
they gave
flowers.
In some places,
sacred smoke
blown to the four
directions.
Some places,
feathers
and good thoughts.
Some places,
fire.

But
everywhere
they knew
to give
something.

And
everywhere
they knew

to turn
their faces
eastward
as the sun
came up.

Some people
still
know.

When the first
pale
streak of light
cuts
through the
darkness,
wherever they are,
those people
make offerings
and send
strong
mysterious
songs
to the sun.

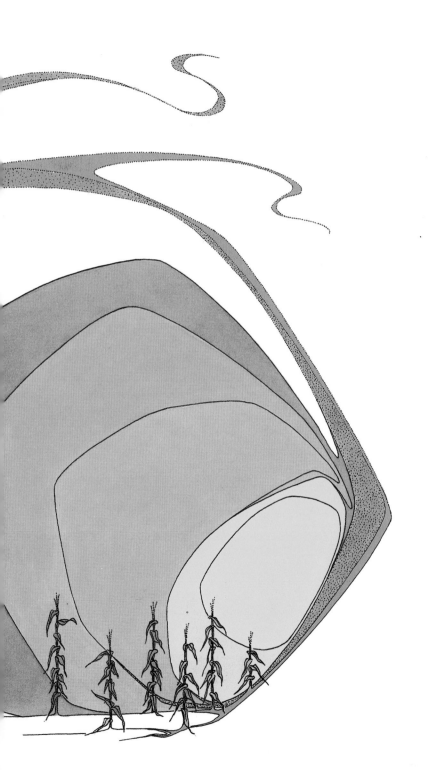

They know
exactly
how to start
a day.

Their blessings
float
on the wind
over
Pueblo cornfields
in New Mexico,
and
you hear
their
morning songs
in villages
in Africa,
and
they salute
the sunrise
ceremonially
in the high
cold mountains
of Peru.

Today
long before dawn
they were
already waiting
in Japan
with prayers
and they were
gathering
at little shrines
in India
with marigolds
in their hands.
They were
bathing
in the sacred
Ganges river
as the sun
came up.

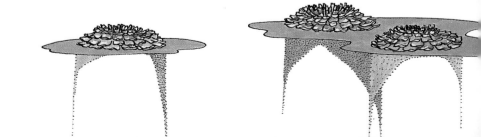

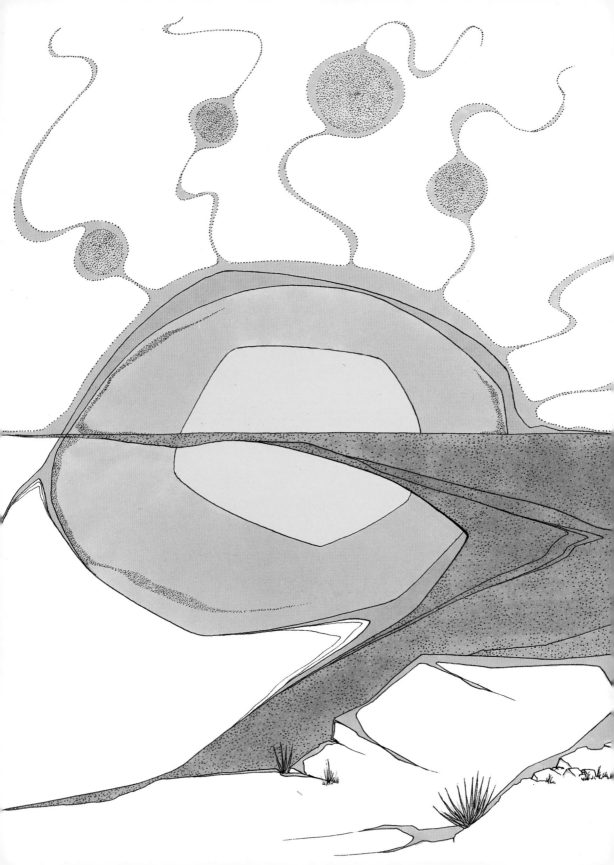

And
high
on a mesa edge
in Arizona
they were holding
a baby
toward the sun.

It had to be
sunrise.
And it had to be
that
first
sudden moment.
That's
when all
the power of
life
is in the
sky.

They were
speaking
the child's
new name
so the sun
would
hear
and know
that child.

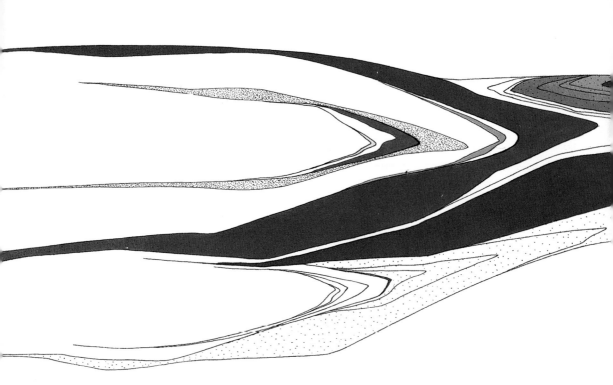

Some people
say
there is
a new sun
every day,
that it
begins
its life
at dawn
and lives
for one day
only.

They say
you have to
welcome it.

You have to
make the sun
happy.
You have to
make
a good day
for it.

You have to
make
a good
world
for it
to live
its
one-day
life in.

And the way to start,
they say,
is just by
looking
east
at dawn.

When they look
east
tomorrow,

you can too.

Your song
will be
an offering—

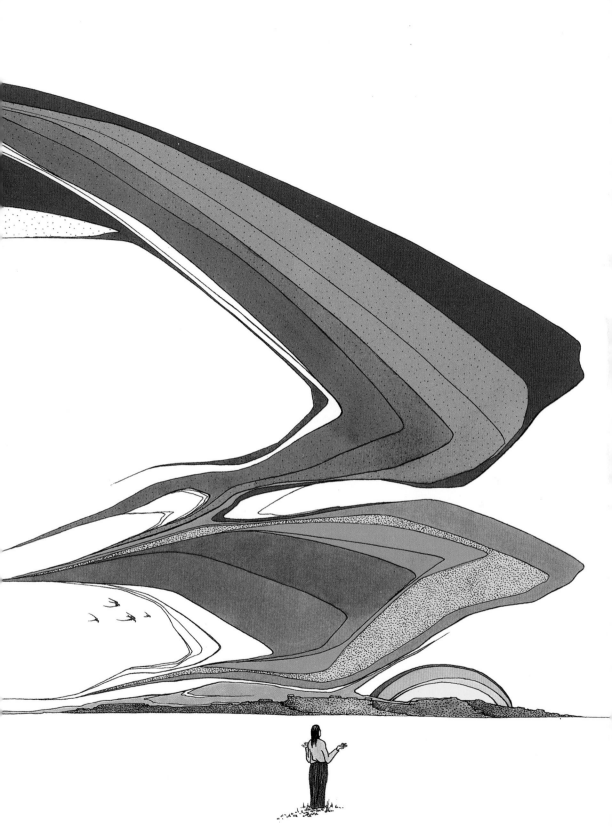

and you'll be
one more person
in one more place
at one more
time
in the world
saying
hello to the sun,
letting it know you are there.

If the sky turns a color
sky never was before

just watch it.

That's part of the magic.
That's the way
to start
a day.